SUPER SNOOP SAM SNOUT
AND THE CASE OF THE MISSING MARBLE

ANNE LeMIEUX

Illustrated by Ray Burns

AN AVON CAMELOT BOOK

SUPER SNOOP SAM SNOUT AND THE CASE OF THE MISSING MARBLE is an original publication of Avon Books. This work has never before appeared in book form.

AVON BOOKS
A division of
The Hearst Corporation
1350 Avenue of the Americas
New York, New York 10019

Text copyright © 1994 by A.C. LeMieux
Illustrations copyright © 1994 by Avon Books
Illustrations by Ray Burns
Published by arrangement with the author
Library of Congress Catalog Card Number: 93-90962
ISBN: 0-380-77460-7
RL: 1.8

First Avon Camelot Printing: June 1994

CAMELOT TRADEMARK REG. U.S. PAT. OFF. AND IN OTHER COUNTRIES, MARCA REGISTRADA, HECHO EN U.S.A.

Printed in the U.S.A.

OPM   10 9 8 7 6 5 4 3 2 1

To The Giff Family
of the Dinosaur's Paw Bookstore
With Love

THIS BOOK
BELONGS TO

Special thanks to Lloyd Ralston
for sharing his antique marbles.

If something smells fishy,
Needs figuring out,
Call the solution sniffer
Super Snoop Sam Snout.

That's me, Samuel William Snyder the Third.

The "Super Snoop" comes from being good at figuring out mysteries.

The "Sam" is my name.

The "Snout" is what Freddy Ruggles calls my nose.

I take after my Gramps, Samuel William Snyder Senior, in name, nose, and occupation.

Gramps used to be a police detective, but he retired for reasons of health. Now he lives on a houseboat in Miami. Sometimes

I consult with him on cases, by telephone, long distance.

I call my latest case The Case of the Missing Marble.

It was springtime.

It was hay fever season. All the pollen in the air was making my nose very stuffy. I had to keep blowing it, which didn't unstuff it, but did make it sore and red.

I was on my way to Tommy Toomey's house for a game of marbles. Tommy has the best yard in the neighborhood for playing marbles. His father is a terrible gardener. Things grow where he doesn't want them to, like weeds in the garden. And things don't grow where he does want them to, like grass in the yard. There are a lot of dirt patches in Tommy's yard. They're perfect for marble matches.

As I passed my mailbox, I saw the flag was up. I flipped it down and took out the mail. Inside, there were two magazines, a booklet of sale coupons for stores in the mall, a ten-million-dollar sweepstakes envelope and a small package wrapped in brown paper. The package was addressed to me.

I ran back into the house and put the mail

on the counter in the kitchen, except for my package. And except for the sweepstakes envelope, which I hid under the phone book to fill out later. My mom always throws them away. She says nobody she knows has ever won a sweepstakes. But I figure somebody has to win, and $10 million could come in handy.

I sat at the table and looked at my package. It was about the size and shape of a paperback book. But it felt heavier than one. Under my name and address, someone had neatly printed FRAGILE—HANDLE WITH CARE—FIRST CLASS in red marker. There was no return address.

But the little round circle stamped on the stamps said *Miami.*

Only one person sends me stuff from Miami—Gramps.

I pulled off the paper and opened the box.

Inside was a note from Gramps. It said, "Hey, Sam, my man, how are you? Hope this helps you shed some light on those cases of yours. Love, Gramps."

Under the note was a brown plastic case. I opened it. Inside was a magnifying glass. A real one. I picked it up. There was a switch on the handle. I flicked it and a little built-in flashlight went on. Now, counting my brain and my Polaroid camera, I had three pieces of real detective equipment.

I decided to bring my new magnifying glass over to Tommy's house to show him.

When I got there, I knocked on Tommy's back door.

"Come on in, Sam," Mrs. Toomey said.

She was sitting at the kitchen table with a lady who looked just like her, very skinny, only shorter, and with the same curly hair, only some white was mixed in with the yellow.

A man was sitting there, too. He was holding a peppermint stick in his mouth like a cigar.

"Sam, these are Tommy's grandparents, Mom-Mom and Pop-Pop. Mom-Mom and Pop-Pop, this is Sam," Mrs. Toomey said.

I was surprised that they were Tommy's grandparents because they didn't look very old. They could have been an aunt and an uncle, or something.

"Hello," I said. "Nice to meet you."

"Oh, isn't Samantha a lovely name for a young girl?" Mom-Mom said.

I touched my head to see if I needed a haircut.

Pop-Pop frowned.

"Sam's a boy, Mother," Mrs. Toomey said.

Mom-Mom squinted.

"Why, yes, of course, Kat-Kat. I was just saying that Samantha IS a lovely name. And don't you start pestering me about glasses again. I can see just fine."

Pop-Pop snorted.

"Tommy's in the den, Sam. Go on out," Mrs. Toomey told me.

I went into the den. Tommy was watching Saturday morning cartoons. He was so tuned into them that he didn't even notice me until I put my magnifying glass right up to his eyeball.

"Yaagh!" Tommy yelled.

I jumped back.

"Oh, sorry," he said. "I thought you were a one-eyed monster."

"You've been watching too many cartoons," I told him. "It's just my new detective magnifying glass with the built-in flashlight. Gramps sent it to me from Miami."

"Hey, that's pretty cool," Tommy said. "Want to see what my grandfather brought me?" he asked.

"Sure," I said.

Tommy got up. We went into the dining room. Tommy's cat, Banshee, was hooked by her claws to the screen in the dining room window. She was trying to get out and eat a family of birds.

Tommy ran over and waved his arms at his cat. "Get down, Banshee! Get off there."

Banshee jumped down, ripping a long gash in the screen. Tommy shook his head and peeked into the kitchen to see if his mother had seen.

"One more rip in that screen won't make much difference," I said.

"My mother said if she sees Banshee on the screen one more time, she's going to chop her up and feed HER to the birds," Tommy said.

Tommy grabbed two sour balls from a candy dish on the dining room table and gave me one.

We went through the living room, and he took two chocolate kisses from another candy dish and gave me one.

"What's with all the candy?" I asked as we went up the stairs to his room.

"It's for Pop-Pop. He has a sweet tooth," Tommy said. "He has to have candy or he gets very cranky. It's great when they come to visit. It's the only time besides Halloween that my mother allows candy in the house.''

''That's not very good for his teeth,'' I said, as we went upstairs.

''It's okay,'' Tommy said. ''Those aren't his teeth.''

''Whose are they?'' I asked.

''I mean, they aren't his own real teeth that he's had since he was a kid,'' Tommy said. ''He can take them out of his mouth.''

We went into Tommy's room. Tommy dragged his chair over to the closet and climbed onto it. He reached up to his closet shelf, moved a stack of games, and pulled out the cigar box that holds his marble collection. Then he climbed down. He sat on the bed and took off the thirty-two rubber bands that he had around the cigar box for extra security.

Inside was the red cloth bag that holds his regular marbles. And the blue cloth bag that holds his shooters. And a bag I'd never seen before that looked very old and soft. It looked like it used to be black but had faded to the color of the lead in a pencil. Tommy picked it up.

"Look-it," he said. He pulled the string loose, opened the bag, and poured five marbles out onto his bed. I went to pick one up.

"Don't touch them," Tommy yelled. I jumped back in case they were exploding marbles, like the golf ball Mr. Ruggles gave to my father when they went golfing together one time.

"They're really old," Tommy said. "Almost a hundred years. They were Pop-Pop's father's when he was a kid."

I knelt down and took out my magnifying glass to get a closer look. Four were clear with thin white swirls in the middle and rainbow-colored swirls around the white ones.

"Those are Philadelphia swirls," Tommy said. "The other one is a green mica."

I examined it. It was clear light green with tiny silver flakes inside. There were two rough spots on the glass.

"I hate to tell you, Tommy, but it looks a little chipped," I told him.

"They're supposed to be that way," Tommy told me. "These are hand-blown glass. Those two rough spots are how you tell."

I turned on the flashlight in my magnifying glass for a better look.

"Oh," I said.

"They're really valuable. I'm starting a collection," Tommy said.

Just then, Banshee came into the room and jumped up on the bed, right in front of my nose. Banshee batted at Tommy's special marbles. I started to sneeze like crazy.

"Get away from my marbles, you dumb cat," Tommy hollered. He shooed her off the bed.

"Want to have a match?" Tommy asked.

"Achoo," I sneezed. Cat hair doesn't help my allergies. "Sure."

Tommy put his special marbles back in their old bag and back in the box. He tucked the box under his arm, put the rubber bands in his pocket, and we went downstairs.

Mom-Mom was in the living room dust

mopping the floor. She bumped into the tall lamp by Mr. Toomey's reading chair.

"Oh, excuse me, Kat-Kat," she said. She reached up and patted the lamp shade. "That's a lovely hat. Are you going out?"

Tommy and I snagged some more candy and headed for the door.

"Mom-Mom needs glasses, but she won't go get her eyes checked," Tommy told me as we went outside.

"How come?" I asked.

"She says glasses would make her look too old. I heard her and Pop-Pop fighting about it last night."

The best marble patch in Tommy's yard is next to the big weed garden under the dining room window. I grabbed a stick and drew two circles for a game of ringtaw. Tommy put his cigar box on some crabgrass behind us.

I won three marbles the first game. Tommy won five marbles the second and third games. That's because the weeds were starting to make me sneeze again.

We started another game so I could win my two marbles back.

Just then, Freddy Ruggles walked up the driveway. He was pushing his baby brother, Teddy Ruggles, in a stroller.

"Hey, Snout," he shouted. "I heard when God was passing out noses, you thought He said 'roses' and said to give you a big red one! Haw-haw!"

"Hey, Freddy, I heard when He was passing out brains, you thought He said 'pains' and told Him not to give you any," I said.

Actually, that's not what I said. But I would have, if I'd thought of it then. For the record, I sneezed two more times.

Tommy and I ignored Freddy and Teddy. We kept on playing.

"Hey, what are these?" Freddy said.

Tommy and I turned around. Freddy was standing on the crabgrass, holding the old marble bag in one hand and Tommy's special hundred-year-old marbles in the other.

"Give me those," Tommy shouted. He jumped up.

Freddy started running around the yard while Tommy and I chased him. He ran through our marble patch and wrecked our game. He ran back and forth across the yard. His brother, Teddy, climbed out of the stroller.

"Those are worth a lot of money, Freddy," Tommy said as he ran. "You better give them back." He chased Freddy toward the weed garden near our marble patch.

"I'm going to tell my mother," Tommy finally shouted.

Freddy stopped running.

"Aw, here, you can have 'em, you big baby." He pretended to hold them out, then turned around and threw them as hard as he could, right at Mr. Toomey's weed garden.

Just then, we heard a funny gurgling sound. We all turned around. Teddy Ruggles was sitting in the middle of our marble patch, rolling something around in his fat cheeks and drooling all over.

"AAAAGH," Freddy yelled. He raced

over, poked his finger in Teddy's mouth and pulled out a yellow marble.

Teddy screamed and started to cry.

"What are you trying to do, choke my brother?" Freddy said.

"Get off my property and take your dopey brother with you," Tommy yelled.

Freddy picked Teddy up. The tears and the drool mixed with the dirt from the marble patch to make this sticky mud that got all over Freddy. It served him right. Freddy stuffed his drooling, muddy baby brother back in the stroller.

"VROOM, VROOM," he said and started racing the stroller down the driveway.

Tommy was looking at the weeds. He looked kind of sick.

"I'll never find them in there," he said.

"We can try. I'll help. Come on," I said. I took out my magnifying glass, turned on the flashlight, and crawled into Mr. Toomey's weed garden.

We looked under every leaf and scrounged around in the dirt. We finally found three of the Philadelphia swirls. I started sneezing like crazy so I had to get out of the weeds. Tommy came out, too.

"Where are the other two?" he said. I looked around. Suddenly I spotted the last

Philadelphia swirl, stuck on the ledge under the dining room window.

"There's one!" I pointed. Tommy plowed through the weeds and got it, while I sneezed some more.

"The green mica's my favorite," Tommy said sadly. "And it's not anywhere."

"It's got to be su-su-CHOO! somewhere," I said. "Can we take a break from looking? These weeds are doing a number on my nose."

We picked up the rest of our regular marbles and sorted them out. Then we went inside and sat down at the kitchen table.

"I bet Freddy stole it," Tommy said. "I bet when he threw the Philadelphia swirls, he held onto the green mica, just to trick me."

"Maybe," I said. "He sure ran away fast."

"Yeah. Just like a crook trying to make

a getaway with the loot. Maybe we should—'' Tommy started to say. Just then, Mom-Mom came into the kitchen.

"Tom-Tom, would you and Sam-Sam like some lunch?" she asked.

Tommy looked embarrassed, like he thought I would be mad about being called Sam-Sam. It didn't bother me. But I felt a little sorry for Tommy. My Gramps would never do something like that in front of one of my friends.

"Want lunch?" Tommy asked.

"Sure. That would be great," I said. "If it's no trouble."

"No trouble at all," Mom-Mom said.

Mom-Mom took a hunk of boloney and a jar of mustard out of the refrigerator. Then she took a loaf of bread from the bread box. She went over to the counter near the sink to make sandwiches. As she sliced the boloney, she sang a song about tiptoeing through tulips. I hoped she could see what she was doing okay. I didn't want part of a finger in my sandwich.

"Mustard for both of you?" she asked.

We both said yes.

In a minute, Mom-Mom brought two baloney sandwiches over to the table.

"There you go, boys." There was a lot of mustard on the outside of my sandwich. I noticed that Mom-Mom had a lot of mustard on her hands, too, even though she'd washed them.

"Thanks, Mom-Mom," Tommy said.

"No trouble, no trouble. You know me. I like to earn my room and board when we visit," Mom-Mom chuckled.

I picked up my sandwich, which I couldn't smell or taste because of my stuffy nose. I took a bite. The whole piece of baloney came out and flapped against my chin. I put it back between the bread and tried to bite harder. The same thing happened again. It was like trying to bite through a piece of rubber. I opened my sandwich and peeked in at the baloney. It was round, flat, and pink. And through the mustard I could see these little letters stamped on it—HANDY DANDY DRAIN STOPPER.

I didn't want to make Tommy feel bad by telling him his grandmother gave me a rubber drain stopper sandwich, so I put it down on the plate.

"Hey, Tommy, I just remembered something I have to go do at home right away," I said. "I'll come back in a little while to help you look for the green mica."

"Okay," Tommy said. He was busy putting all the rubber bands back on his cigar box.

I went home and made myself a peanut butter sandwich. When I was nibbling the last bit of good part out of the crust, the phone rang. I answered it.

"Hey, Sam, my man. You sound like you have quite a cold there." It was Gramps, long distance, from Miami.

"Not a cold," I told him. "Hay fever. Catch any fish lately?"

I always ask him that. He fishes all the time, but his doctor won't let him use any bait. His doctor says the excitement of catching a fish might be too much of a strain on his health.

"No, no. Can't catch a fish without bait," Gramps said, the way he always does. "Got my fishing line tangled up with the fishing line of a mighty fine-looking neighbor lady, though. Heh, heh, could be I caught something special this time. Speaking of special, anything special in the mail lately?"

"Yeah, I got it this morning. Thanks a million, Gramps. I already used it to track down some missing property." I told him about Tommy's marbles.

"Still one missing, eh? Well, according to Einstein, matter can't just disappear into thin air for no good reason," Gramps said.

So I told him about our suspect.

"That old Freddy Ruggles again, eh?"

Gramps said. "With an accomplice. Well, Sam, my man, accusing someone of stealing is a serious thing. You better make mighty sure of your facts."

"Okay, Gramps. I will. And thanks again," I said. I hung up.

I went up to my room and found a notebook from school that was only half used

CRIME- STOLEN (maybe) MARBLE

DESCRIPTION- SMALL (not shooter) GREEN MICA

VICTIM- TOMMY TOOMEY

SUSPECT NUMBER 1 - FREDDY RUGGLES

up. I ripped out the used pages and started making a list.

I chewed on my pencil eraser for a minute. I tried to come up with some more ideas about what might have happened.

Teddy Ruggles tried to eat a yellow marble. Maybe when we were chasing Freddy around the yard, he dropped the green mica on our marble patch. Maybe before Teddy put the yellow one into his mouth, he put the green one into his mouth.

Maybe Teddy Ruggles ATE the green mica! That would make it very hard to recover.

"SUSPECT NUMBER 2—TEDDY RUGGLES," I wrote.

I couldn't think of anything else. I decided to return to the scene of the crime.

Tommy was in the kitchen, eating Chocadoodle-Doo Bars with Pop-Pop.

"So did you think of anything?" Tommy asked.

"I'm still working on it," I said. I opened the Chocadoodle-Doo Bar he handed me and tried to picture what happened once more. Freddy threw the marbles right at that weed garden. One landed on the dining room windowsill.

Just then, Mom-Mom came in from the dining room.

"Tommy Toomey, you better teach that cat of yours some manners. She knocked Pop-Pop's candy dish right off the dining room table," Mom-Mom said.

"Sorry, Mom-Mom," Tommy said. "I'll go pick up the candy."

"I already did," Mom-Mom said.

I looked at Mom-Mom. A new idea popped into my head.

"Do you mind if I snoop around a little?" I asked Tommy.

"Go ahead," he said.

It was worth a try. Otherwise we'd have to go tell Mrs. Ruggles that her son Teddy needed an operation to get the marble out of his stomach. Or that her son Freddy

wasn't only a creep and a bully, he was a real thief.

I went into the dining room. I took out my magnifying glass and turned on the flashlight. I examined the candy dish. Some of the sour balls had yellow dust on them. I moved some of the pieces around to look underneath. I saw a shiny green sour ball with silver flecks in it—Tommy's green mica!

I picked it out of the bowl, being careful not to wipe off the yellow dust.

I went back into the kitchen.

"Here it is," I said and held it up. "The missing marble."

Tommy was amazed. "Did Freddy bring it back?" he asked.

"Freddy didn't take it," I told him. "But he did throw it. Remember we found one Philadelphia swirl on the dining room win-

dow ledge? Well, this one went right through one of Banshee's screen holes. It must have landed on the floor. Then Banshee knocked over the dish of sour balls. When Mom-Mom was picking them up, she found the marble and thought it was candy. She put it back in the dish. See the yellow powder? Dried mustard. Mom-Mom, can I see your hands?"

Mom-Mom held out her hands. Across

one knuckle was a dried glob of mustard from when she made our baloney and drain stopper sandwiches.

"How terribly embarrassing," Mom-Mom said. She went over to the sink to wash her hands again. She came back and sat down and squinted at her hands.

"Is it all gone now? I can't really see very well," she said.

She looked sad. I felt bad. Pop-Pop reached over and took both of her hands in his.

"I think you'd look beautiful in glasses. What do you say, Momsy?" he said.

Then Mom-Mom smiled. "I say I guess we better take a quick trip over to Eyes R Us. I think maybe it's time I got some glasses."

When I got home, I called Gramps to let him know how my case turned out.

"Well, Sam, my man, you sure mustered up some smarts to figure that one out," Gramps said.

It's good to know I can sniff out the answer to a mystery even when my sniffer's so stuffed I can't smell a thing.